NEN
AND THE LONELY FISHERMAN

To my husband - IE

For Toto, with love - JM

ISBN: 978-1-913339-09-8

Text copyright – Ian Eagleton 2021

Illustrations copyright – James Mayhew 2021

Cover design by Ness Wood

NEN
AND THE LONELY FISHERMAN

Ian Eagleton

James Mayhew

First published in the UK 2021 by Owlet Press

www.owletpress.com

Far out to sea, deep below the whispering waves,
there once lived a merman called Nen.

Nen loved exploring

the ancient, wild depths —

the gliding fish,

the shimmering sand,

and the ghostly, sunken ships.

But something was missing.

His heart felt ... empty.

So, at night, Nen sang a sad song and the twinkling stars whispered his words of hope across the ocean. But Nen's song was smothered by heavy clouds, and he returned to the seabed alone.

Every night, Nen's father, Pelagios, watched his son leave their underwater kingdom.
And every night, he pleaded with him to stay away from the world above.

But Nen ignored
his father's warnings.

As he began to explore the world beyond his own, Nen noticed rows of fishing boats bobbing on the waves. And just beyond those fishing boats, there lived a lonely fisherman called Ernest.

He spent his days rescuing ...

freeing ...

collecting ...

dreaming ...

and creating!

But every night, Ernest gazed out to sea and wondered
if something more was waiting for him, just beyond the horizon.

Then one still, clear night, he heard something drifting over the sighing ocean.
Something beautiful and mysterious ...

It was Nen's song! It was so tender and brimming with such courage that a long-forgotten feeling stirred inside the lonely fisherman's heart.

Filled with excitement, Ernest set off to find out who this magical voice belonged to.

He searched and searched the swirling sea-waves and
became aware of something, someone, hiding just out of sight ...

A ripple ...

A shimmer ...

A flicker ...

Could it be ...?

The silver moon shone down on Nen's hair and glittering salt-splash jewels made Ernest's eyes sparkle. As the soft night-time breeze wrapped around them, they both felt their hope turn to happiness.

His face etched with worry, Pelagios begged his son again to stay away from the humans in the world above. They were destroying his precious oceans!

But Nen knew that Ernest was different ...

So, he returned each night to see him in his rickety boat. Together, they would talk and laugh and dream while the skies changed from a golden amber to an inky purple.

One night, as Nen swam back to his hidden world, far beneath the ocean's surface, Pelagios could no longer control his frustration …

Tears of anger and sadness began to fall, and great clouds gathered. Thunder roared. Splinters of lightning were flung across the sky.

Poor Ernest was thrown from his rickety boat into the raging sea!

Nen fought through the churning, lashing tempest, in a desperate search for his fisherman.

Down,

down,

down, he swam . . .

into the dark depths of the ocean.

But there was no sign of Ernest.

Nen struggled upwards through the violent waves.
Suddenly, he spotted something just out of reach ...

ERNEST!

He was battered by the waves, broken and lifeless.

As the sea slowly calmed and the hazy sun peeked through the clouds, Nen carried his fisherman to the shore.

He waited ...

And waited …

To his relief, Ernest finally woke with a cough and a splutter.
He smiled, looking up into Nen's worried eyes.

Pelagios wondered if perhaps,
just maybe,
Ernest was different after all ...

Now, as he looks out across the calm sea, Ernest is no longer lonely.

With a splash and a flick of a tail, Nen is there, waiting by the shore!

And under each dazzling blue sky, while the seagulls dive and squawk,
Nen and Ernest hold hands, laughing and dreaming about the future.

DISCOVER MORE STORIES TO TREASURE

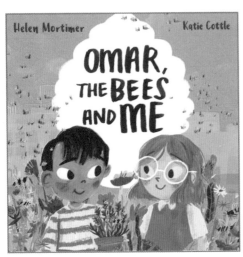

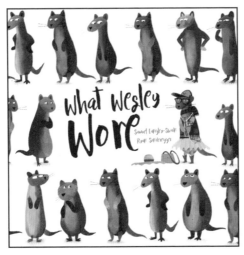

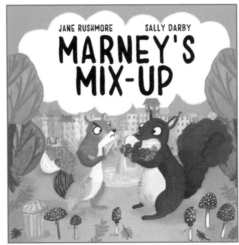

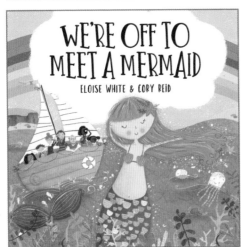

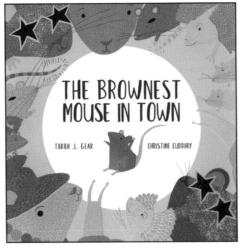

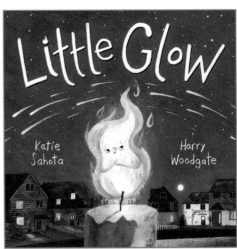

Follow **@owletpress** on social media or visit **www.owletpress.com** to learn more about us.